My Second C

The Friends to Lo

by

Reba Bale

Table of Contents

Prologue—Vickie 1

Claire 3

Vickie 6

Claire 10

Vickie 14

Claire 19

Vickie 23

Claire 27

Vickie 31

Claire 35

Vickie 38

Claire 42

Vickie 47

Claire 51

Epilogue – Vickie 55

Special Preview 58

Other Books by Reba Bale 62

Copyright

About This Book

Eleven years ago, they were one of the first lesbian couples to be married in Seattle. Ten years ago, they got divorced. Or so they thought...

Claire Langford has a big problem. She wants to marry her girlfriend, but when they apply for a marriage license, she's shocked to learn that she's still married to her first wife, Vickie. It was love at first sight when the two women met, but once they were married, they learned they were just too different to make it long-term.

Vickie McMaster never got over her first wife. Her only wife. She'd been devastated when Claire served her with divorce papers, unwilling to work through their problems. So, when the only woman she's ever loved shows up on her doorstep demanding that she sign new divorce papers, Vickie devises a plan.

She's going to convince Claire to give their love a second chance at forever, even if it means she has to play dirty...

"My Second Chance" is book twelve in the "Friends to Lovers" romantic novella series. Each book in the series is a steamy standalone featuring an LGBTQ couple making the leap from friends to lovers and looking for their "happily ever after".

Be sure to check out a free preview of Reba Bale's lesbian romance "The Divorcee's First Time" at the end of this book!

Dedication

For second chances: the ones you never got, the ones you got but didn't work out (at least you tried), and for the ones that brought a happily ever after.

Join My Newsletter

Want a free book? Join my newsletter and you'll receive a fun subscriber gift. I promise I will only email you when there are new releases or special sales, usually twice a month.

Visit my newsletter sign-up page at bit.ly/RebaBaleSapphic[2] to join today.

Prologue—Vickie

Ten years ago...

"I can't believe you're doing this." I lifted my tear-filled eyes to stare across the table at the woman I loved. The woman who I thought loved me too. "There's got to be something we can do to fix this. Counseling maybe?"

Claire was shaking her head before I even finished my question.

"Vickie, we've been over this. Getting married was a mistake. We both bought into the fantasy that people could fall in love at first sight and live happily ever after. Then we let ourselves get swept away in the gay marriage rush. But with all that behind us, it's clear that we don't have a lot in common and we want very different things in life."

She pointed at the stack of papers sitting on the table. "Sign the divorce papers and we ca both get on with our lives before we hurt each other anymore than we already have."

I was full-on sobbing now. Love should be enough. Sure, we'd had a lot of bumps in our first year of marriage, but didn't everyone?

She was right, we were very different people. I was an artist and a musician. As an activist and a free spirit, I didn't worry much about things like retirement accounts and social norms.

Claire, on the other hand, was a planner. A business person. Her mind was analytical and logical, and appearances were very important to her. She embarrassed easily, and one of the things that seemed to embarrass her the most was me.

It hadn't always been this way. We met fifteen months ago at a music festival on Whidbey Island, and it was love at first sight. Both of us had come with friends, and I noticed her right away, probably because she'd come wearing khakis and a button-down shirt like she'd just gotten off work at an audit firm or something. I'd walked right up to her and asked her to dance.

She took one look at my tiny tie-dye dress and bare feet and given me the most beautiful smile.

"*Yes, I'd love to dance with you,*" she'd said in the slightly snooty voice she had. I knew now that she'd gotten that voice from her mother, the queen of the snooty people. Although after a year of me charming her, Mrs. Langford was finally starting to warm up to me.

Claire came home with me that first night and pretty much never left. Two months later we were walking hand in hand past City Hall when we saw a line of people waiting outside the courthouse.

***

"*Oh, that's right, today's the first day that same sex couples can legally be married in Washington,*" she said. "*I never thought I'd see the day.*"

"*It's fate that we're walking by right now,*" I declared, pulling her into the line.

"*What? Fate? What are you talking about?*"

"*The voters of Washington State have given us the same rights as the heteros, and we just happen to walk by right as they're issuing the first marriage licenses? I say we celebrate that right by getting married. Right now.*"

"*You're crazy,*" Claire laughed, even though I could tell she was thinking about it.

"*I dare you to ask me to marry you,*" I said.

My girlfriend was very competitive, and I'd quickly learned that she could never resist a dare.

"*I dare you to say yes,*" she retorted.

"*Yes.*"

Claire

"What do you mean they won't issue the marriage license?"

I frowned at the phone even though my fiancée Susannah couldn't see me.

"They said you're still married. That's crazy, right?"

Her tone of voice made it clear that I'd better agree with her.

"Of course."

"This says you married a Victoria McMaster on December ninth twenty-twelve. My attorney pulled the marriage license from the County records and it's your date of birth and your signature, Claire."

I had a sinking feeling in my stomach as I realized that I'd never mentioned to Susannah that I'd been married before. I don't know why, it was so long ago, and the marriage was so short that it didn't count, right? Or at least that's how I justified it to myself.

Susannah's voice turned sharp. "Is there something you want to tell me, Claire?"

Oh damn it, she sounded really mad.

"Can we talk about it tonight?" I asked.

"I'd like to talk about it now." Her tone brooked no argument.

"Um. Well, funny story. When I was younger, I dated this woman Vickie and we fancied ourselves in love. We were young and impulsive, you know how you are in your twenties, and we sort of got married on a whim."

"The LGBTQ community fought for years to get the right to marry, and you got married on a whim?" she screeched.

Susannah was a screecher.

"Yeah." I couldn't defend myself on that point. "I mean, we were walking by City Hall the day they started issuing licenses and we got caught up in all the excitement."

3

"In the two years that we've been dating, including the six months that we've been engaged, you never thought to mention it?" Susannah asked.

"It was a very short marriage."

"What, like a week?"

"No, more like a year. Well, fourteen months. But I'm not married to her anymore, honestly. We got divorced like ten years ago."

"Not according to the state of Washington you didn't."

I winced. "This is all a mistake, I promise. I'll contact the attorney who handled the divorce and get this cleared up right away."

"I hope so. Mother is going to be furious if something delays the wedding."

Susannah's mother was furious on a weekly basis, pretty much any time the world didn't bend to her will. She was old money, rich and snobby, and she did not abide by anything interfering with her plans. She was a bitch, honestly, and I had to admit that from time to time my fiancée exhibited some behavior that reminded me of her mother in an unflattering way.

The wedding planning had definitely brought out an unpleasant side of her that felt like a huge red flag.

I squashed that uncharitable thought and returned my focus to Susannah.

"Mother says we won't be able to get a new date at the country club if you can't clear this up. She already had to pull a lot of strings to get us in. They're booked out like five years for weddings."

"Don't worry, Susannah," I said soothingly. I did a lot of soothing with my fiancée, truth be told. "I promise you I can fix this."

Two hours later I realized that fixing it was going to be a little more complicated than I anticipated.

"What do you mean the papers were never filed?" I asked incredulously.

The attorney on the phone chuckled nervously. "Well, my father was representing you, and right after you signed the papers, he had a heart attack and was out of the office for several months. It appears that someone thought the papers had been filed before he got sick, because they stamped the originals with 'copy' and filed them in a cabinet."

"We can just file them now then, right?" I asked.

"I'm afraid it's not that simple, Ms. Langford. Even if we could get the court clerk to accept papers marked 'copy', which is highly unlikely, the signatures are ten years old. Generally, they only recognize papers that are signed within one hundred and twenty days or less. There's no judge in the county who will accept these papers like they are. I'm terribly sorry for the inconvenience, but you're going to need to re-file. We won't charge you, of course, since it was our error."

"Fine," I huffed. "What do I need to do to re-file?"

"I can draw up new papers that are compliant with today's divorce laws, and then you and your wife—."

"Ex-wife," I interrupted.

The attorney wisely chose not to argue. "You'll both need to sign and notarize the papers. I can get them prepared by the end of the week. Do you want to hire someone to serve Ms. McMaster, or do you want to serve them personally?"

"I'd better go myself," I said reluctantly. "I need to explain what happened. Can you find an address for me? I haven't talked to her since we split up ten years ago, and I have no idea where to find her."

"I'll take care of it, Ms. Langford."

Vickie

"That's a beautiful picture, Jayden."

The seven year old gave me a big smile, revealing a gap where his two front teeth used to be.

"Thank you, Miss Vickie."

I saw Jayden's adoptive mother standing in the doorway of my home studio and waved her in.

"Hi Marielle, come see what Jayden made today."

After Marielle gushed over the photo, I led her out to the waiting area to give her a quick update on my session with Jayden. I had a very busy practice as an art therapist, where I used art and music to help kids with trauma histories or developmental challenges grow in confidence and develop social skills and the ability to form relationships.

Jayden was one of my favorite stories. Rescued from an abusive home, he'd been non-verbal when he'd gone into foster care with Marielle. After his mother was sentenced to life in prison, Marielle and her wife applied for adoption, and by all reports, Jayden had thrived under their care. I'd seen incredible progress since we'd started working together.

"How was he today?" my client's mother asked.

"He was good. I got him to open up about his fear of sleeping with the light off and encouraged him to talk to you and Amanda about his issues with it tonight."

Marielle nodded. "Great, thank you so much Vickie, we'll see you next week."

After walking them to their car, I headed across the lawn to my house. One of the reasons that I'd purchased this property in the Seattle suburbs was the large 'granny flat' in the yard that I was able to convert into an office for my practice. It made for a short commute.

As I came around the corner of my house, I saw a man standing on the porch.

"Can I help you?"

"Victoria McMaster?" he said formally.

Oh god, I hoped I wasn't being sued or something. It was every therapist's worst nightmare, and the reason our liability insurance was so high. Whoever this guy was, he had first-year attorney written all over him.

"Yes."

He gave me what passed for a smile. "My name is David Willis, I represent your grandmother, Elizabeth McMaster."

I couldn't help the stab of pain in my gut at the mention of the grandmother I hadn't seen in twenty years.

"Is she dead?" I asked. "And how did you find me?"

After a disastrous coming out, I'd run away from home at fifteen and never talked to any of my family since then. I wasn't on social media and kept all of my personal information private.

"I'm not sure, ma'am. I was just asked to give you this letter."

He shoved the envelope into my hands and took off at a brisk pace, not even bothering to say goodbye. Filled with trepidation, I sat on the front step and skimmed the letter.

My dearest Victoria,

I hope this letter finds you well. I've been looking for you for several years now. I know I treated you terribly when you came out to me and your parents, and I don't have any excuse for that, other than it was a very different time and we didn't understand things like that the way we do now. My private investigator found this newspaper clipping that finally helped us find you. Congratulations on your wedding, you both look very happy.

Can we talk sometime? Please. I know I don't deserve your forgiveness, but I'm asking for it anyway. I just turned ninety, and I don't have much time left. I'd like to spend what little time I have left getting to know my granddaughter again. I love and miss you. Nana

There was a phone number at the bottom of the letter, one that I recognized as the phone number she'd had when I was younger. I guess that Nana never got rid of her landline.

Underneath the letter was a copy of a newspaper article that made my stomach cramp in pain for the second time in five minutes.

Couples Line Up to Be the First to Marry Under State's New Gay Marriage Law

There, front and center, was a photo of me and my ex-wife Claire. We looked young and happy, with our arms around each other's waist. I skimmed the article, seeing that we were also quoted in it.

"It means everything to us to be able to get married like everyone else," said Claire Langford, 25. "I'm marrying the love of my life today."

Langford and girlfriend Vickie McMaster were the seventeenth couple in King County to receive a marriage license under the new law.

I hadn't thought about Claire or my grandmother in several years. I'd moved on with my life after my separation from each of them, and I made it a practice never to look back. I re-read my grandmother's letter.

Nana had hurt me deeply when I came out to my family, going so far as to call me an abomination. I'd half expected that reaction from my parents, but my grandmother and I had always been so close, I figured that she would look past any prejudices about the LGBTQ community. I ran away the next day, ending up in a youth shelter in Seattle where I was able to finish school and eventually move out on my own.

My grandmother had made the first step, I guess it couldn't hurt to call her. The truth was, I was curious about what she wanted to say to me, and how she was doing.

Fifteen minutes later I was wrapping up a stilted but bittersweet conversation with my grandmother. I'd almost burst into tears when she told me that she'd kept her landline phone all these years in case I ever tried to call her.

"Victoria dear, do you think you can come visit me sometime? And bring your beautiful wife. I'd love to meet her."

"Wife?" It took me a second to realize who she was talking about. "Claire?"

"Yes, she looked like a nice girl in the picture. I was so glad that you'd found someone to settle down with."

The easy acceptance of my marriage was something I hadn't expected.

"Well, the thing is..."

"I'm sorry dear, but my home nurse is here now, and I need to talk to her. Can we talk again soon?"

"Sure. How about I call you tomorrow?"

"I'd like that."

I hung up with my grandmother feeling nostalgic. She told me that she'd been looking for me ever since my parents died in a car accident five years ago. Her church had been welcoming LGBTQ couples for many years, and losing my parents made her realize how something like my being a lesbian shouldn't be a barrier to a relationship.

I wasn't sure how I felt about it all, but I figured I would talk to her, maybe go up to Vancouver for a visit, and see how it went.

Putting down the phone, I headed into the kitchen in search of a bottle of wine. After all the emotions associated with hearing from someone in my past, I needed a drink.

Claire

I glanced around curiously as I parked my car in the long driveway in front of Vickie's house. A small sign at the entrance said, *Victoria McMaster, ATR*. I wasn't sure what it meant, but I saw a separate building set back from the house that looked like an office of some sort.

That was different. When Vickie and I were together, she was an artist and a musician, never interested in a 'day job'. She always teased me about being chained to a desk all day and working 'for the man', although technically my boss was a super powerful female billionaire.

Given that it was almost five thirty, I decided to try the house first. Vickie lived in an adorable Craftsman cottage, with a riot of flowers growing in raised gardens along the front of the house and along the sidewalk to the porch. Vickie had always loved to garden, but back when we were together we lived in an apartment with no yard. She'd set up a container garden on the balcony instead.

Grabbing my bag, I glanced quickly in the rear-view mirror to make sure there was nothing on my face, then headed up to the porch. I rang the doorbell, waiting as I heard someone call out, "Coming!"

Vickie threw open the front door and we both froze.

She looked almost exactly the same as I remembered. She was tall and slim with long reddish brown hair, clear pale skin, high cheekbones, and dark brown eyes framed by thick, dark eyebrows. She was wearing faded blue jeans and a peasant blouse that was unbuttoned just enough to reveal that she was a bit curvier than she'd been back when we were together.

I'd forgotten how beautiful she was. A pang of lust rolled through me.

My soon-to-be ex-wife stared at me. "Is it blast from the past day or something?"

"Hi Vickie," I said politely, like I was there to sell her insurance. "How have you been?"

"What are you doing here, Claire?"

Her face morphed into a neutral mask. It used to be that every emotion Vickie ever had would show on her face, but now I couldn't read her at all.

"I need to talk to you about something. It's important. Do you mind if I come in?"

She sighed. "I guess."

She turned around, muttering something about who else from the past was going to show up next.

I walked through the doorway, reeling with the conflicting emotions I was feeling. It was like something settled inside me for the first time in ten years the minute I laid eyes on Vickie. But that was ridiculous. I was engaged to...um, what's her name.

"I was just about to have a glass of wine," Vickie called over her shoulder. "Do you want one?"

"Sure."

I followed her through the house, my eyes bouncing around as I took in her house. It was colorful and arty but stylish, with what looked like high-end touches. When we entered the kitchen, I couldn't help but notice the expensive stainless steel appliances. Whatever Vickie did now, she must be making good money.

"Have a seat."

I settled at the kitchen table as Vickie opened a bottle of wine, grabbing two glasses and bringing them to the table with a bottle of what looked like a nice merlot. She poured us each an almost full glass, took a large sip from hers, then pinned me with a stare.

"Out with it. Why are you here after ten years of radio silence?"

I took a sip of my own liquid courage before I responded.

"Funny thing, I found out recently that we're not really divorced."

"What?" Her voice turned a little high, and I winced.

"Yeah, long story short, our attorney had some medical issues and never filed the papers with the court." I shrugged. "Looking back, we should have received papers confirming that the divorce was final, but I forgot all about it once we split up."

"So what? You're going to file the divorce papers now? You could have emailed me all this."

I tried not to feel hurt that she obviously didn't want to see me. It made sense. I'd been the one to initiate the divorce.

"Well, we can't file them now because the signatures are too old and some of the state laws have changed over the last ten years. So we need to re-file. I had my attorney draw up new papers for us."

I pulled a large manilla envelope out of my bag.

"It's a little more complicated now because we both own property, so we need to do a declaration of assets. And my attorney warned me that depending on which judge we get, we might be asked to go to mediation, although given our long separation, he's hopeful we can waive that part."

"Mediation? Washington is a no-fault divorce state."

"I know, but it will make everything go faster if we just jump through the hoops."

"Faster?" she asked. "We've been separated for ten years, what's the rush?"

"I'm getting remarried," I said. "And there's a mandatory ninety day 'cooling off' period before a divorce can be finalized, so I don't have a lot of time to get this all taken care of."

A flash of pain crossed Vickie's face before she schooled her expression again.

"I see." She took a bracing sip of wine, then her eyes went to a piece of paper on the table. She stared at it thoughtfully and when she looked at me again, I had a bad feeling.

"If you want me to sign these new divorce papers so you can get remarried, I'm going to need a favor from you too."

Our eyes met and held, and I felt a rush of emotions I couldn't quite interpret.

"What kind of a favor?" I asked cautiously.

"I'm going to need you to come to Vancouver with me to visit my grandmother."

"Why?" I asked.

"She invited the two of us to come for a weekend. She thinks we're still married."

"Technically we *are* still married," I reminded her unnecessarily.

"She's hoping to see me living my happily ever after with my wife before she dies. If you don't want me to contest this divorce, you're going to help me give her that."

Vickie

The expression on Claire's face was priceless.

"I...um...what are you talking about?" she asked. "I thought you were estranged from your family."

I got distracted for a second looking at her face. Claire was a classic beauty, with pale white skin, long blonde hair pulled back in a sleek ponytail, and bright blue eyes. She was dressed in a light gray blouse and darker gray pencil skirt that fell to her knees, the perfect little business woman. She'd put on a few pounds over the last few years, the youthful leanness replaced with some banging curves that I wished I could get my hands on.

The truth was, part of me was still in love with Claire, although I hadn't realized it until this very minute.

I'd never been able to connect with any other woman the way I had with her and believe me that I'd tried. I found myself comparing every single woman I dated to the woman I'd married, and undoubtedly, they fell short.

The first time I ever saw Claire I'd known instinctively that she was my soulmate, and as much as I wanted to believe that was just some romantic notion of my youthful self, it wasn't. When I saw her standing on my porch I knew: I was still in love with her, and no matter what happened, I always would be.

Maybe I was an asshole asking her to go to Vancouver with me, but it would kill two birds with one stone. First, it would help me avoid disappointing my Nana on our first visit together in twenty years. And second, it would give me time to win her back.

She might be engaged to that other woman, but she was married to me.

"My grandmother recently reconnected to me, partly because a private investigator found this." I handed her the copy of the newspaper article, and her eyes softened in memory. "I talked to her today for the first time since I was fifteen, and she made a point of saying how she wants to meet my beautiful wife. That would be you, by the way. She was so excited that I was married, I'm not going to break the news to her on our first meeting that my wife abandoned me years ago."

"I didn't abandon you," Claire protested.

I felt my left eyebrow rise to my hairline as I pinned her with a hard stare.

"You decided that our marriage was a mistake, and you made no effort to figure out how we could fix it. You didn't even want to talk about it. Instead, you handed me divorce papers and walked out the door."

Unlike me, Claire had family to go back to when we split up.

"It was a mistake to get married," Claire said, although something in her tone made me think she was trying to convince both of us. "We were young and foolish and overly romantic. We were way too different to make things work long-term."

"You mean I was too weird for your stuck-up family and your snobby rich friends."

It was an old argument, one we'd had many times. Claire went off script though.

"I was way too concerned about material things and appearances back then, that's true," she said, her tone conciliatory. "But all that aside, we weren't compatible."

"We were very compatible in the bedroom," I reminded her.

I'd never had such intense and satisfying sexual encounters until I met Claire. And I hadn't since then either.

"Come with me to my grandmother's, play the part of the happy wife, and then when we get back, I'll sign your divorce papers," I offered. "Do this one thing for me Claire, that's all I ask."

I wasn't being entirely truthful. Sure, I didn't want to disappoint my grandmother, but I also knew instinctively that this would be my one chance to rekindle my relationship with Claire. And I intended to pull out all the stops to make it happen.

I didn't fight for her then, but I sure as hell wasn't going to give up as easily this time.

***

Two weeks later...

"Why does she need to come here to my house? I offered to pick you up."

My home was my sanctuary, and there was no way I wanted Claire's girlfriend to invade it. I knew, just knew, that she was going to be a bitch. Maybe it was jealousy, but I'd always had good intuition about these things.

I could practically hear Claire's eyes rolling through the phone. "I don't think it's that weird for my fiancé to want to meet the woman I'm going away with for the weekend," she said.

My grandmother lived in a city called Vancouver, a small city that was a three-hour drive from Seattle, located right across the river from Portland, Oregon.

My grandmother had been beyond thrilled when I told her that we were going to come for a visit. After some debate, Claire and I decided to leave on a Friday morning, spend the weekend with Nana, then come back on Monday afternoon.

I'd spoken with my grandmother's nurse who told me that Nana was pretty frail and would likely only be able to visit with us for short periods of time each day because she got tired easily. I'd gone years not knowing if my grandmother was dead or alive, but now that I knew she was alive, it made me sad that her health was failing. I wondered how much being alone had exacerbated her condition. My grandfather died before I was even born, and when my parents died, that left her alone other than some distant cousins.

I woke up early on Friday, packing up the car for our road trip, then settled on the porch to wait for Claire to get here. Right at ten a.m. a silver Mercedes pulled into the drive, two women seated in the front seat.

Claire stepped out with a tentative smile, wearing a casual sundress and sandals in a nod to the forecasted ninety degree temperatures in Washington today. She looked much softer than she had the day she'd come over to my house.

Her fiancée looked like just the kind of woman I would have imagined Claire ending up with. She was tall and almost painfully thin, with perfectly coifed platinum hair pulled into a twist at the back of her head. She was wearing a silk dress, three-inch heels that could easily be used as a weapon, and a strand of pearls like she was a senator's wife in some southern state instead of a lesbian in the progressive city of Seattle.

I hated her on site.

The fiancée looked around, her mouth curled up in distaste as if I lived in a tenement instead of a very cute suburban house on a corner lot.

"Susannah, this is my ex-wife, Vickie." Claire's eyes dared me to contradict the 'ex-wife' part. "Vickie, this is my fiancée, Susannah Johanson."

"It's a pleasure to meet you, Vickie." Susannah's voice said otherwise. Her cold dead eyes told me that she had men on speed dial who would gut me like a fish and make it so no one could find the body.

"Susie, so nice to meet you." I approached her with a big, fake smile and reached for her hand. It was like shaking hands with a dead fish.

I wasn't sure why I was so fixated on fish this morning, maybe my body was telling me that I needed to get more omega oils in my diet. The thought made me smirk.

"It's Susannah," she corrected me.

I shrugged like I didn't give a shit – probably because I didn't—and turned to Claire.

"Are you ready to go on our road trip, wifey?"

Susannah's face turned red with rage, but she kept her mouth shut.

"I'll call you tonight," Claire promised her fiancée. "See you Monday when I get back."

I noticed that Claire didn't kiss her goodbye.

Claire

"Did you have to do that?" I asked as we loaded my bag into the trunk of Vickie's car. It was a dark blue Subaru, which was the official car of both Washingtonians and lesbians.

"Do what?"

"Bait Susannah with that wifey comment?"

Vickie shrugged. "Technically it's true."

I ground my teeth together. Susannah was beyond upset that I was accompanying Vickie on this trip, and I didn't appreciate the way she was holding the divorce over my head to get what she wanted. I wasn't sure what Vickie wanted exactly, but I had no doubt she was up to something.

"It's a long drive," she said. "Why don't we try to catch up on the last ten years? My grandmother will expect us to know stuff about each other, what with being married for the last eleven years and all."

I crossed my arms and slid down low in my seat. "Fine."

I knew I was acting like a brat, but I didn't care. I should have eaten breakfast.

As if she knew that I was cranky because I was hungry, Vickie reached behind the passenger seat, rooting around in her bag and pulling out an apple. She handed it to me without a word.

"Tell me about your job," she said.

"I'm still at Phoenix Software, same as when we were together," I said, taking a big bite of my apple. "I manage our Employee Solutions team now."

"You were team lead when they started it, right?"

"Yes, that's right," I responded, pleased that she'd remembered.

"You must like it there to stay in one place all these years."

"Yeah, the company is a great place to work, and my boss has been very good to me over the years. But what about you?" I asked. "What kind of work are you doing now? I saw your sign in the driveway, but I don't know what it means."

"I'm a registered art therapist. I work with kids who've had a lot of traumatic experiences, or kids that don't fit in well due to things like neurodivergence, and teach them how to tap into their emotions through art and music."

I swung my head to stare at her. "Don't you need a psychology degree or something for that?"

She nodded as she pulled onto the entrance ramp for Interstate 5, the road we'd take all the way down to Vancouver.

"I minored in psychology in undergrad, then after we split up, I went to grad school and got a master's in counseling with a specialization in art therapy."

"Wow," I said, impressed. "You do well with that, I take it?"

Vickie frowned. "Everything isn't about money, Claire, but yes, my work pays me well enough to live comfortably. More importantly, it's very fulfilling and I get to help people."

This was an old argument, that I was too focused on money and appearances. The truth was that I'd moved away from all that after we divorced, but these last two years with Susannah had brought an awareness of status back into my life that I was only now realizing was a bit snobbish.

Maybe more than a bit...I'd seen the way Susannah looked around Vickie's property with an expression like she'd smelled dog shit. For some reason, it made me feel protective of Vickie. It was obvious she'd worked hard in her career and was proud of her place.

As we headed south, our conversation got easier until we were talking and laughing like old times. We stopped in Centralia, a small town just off the interstate, to fill up the gas tank and get some lunch. I'd burned through that apple pretty quick.

"Let's go to Burgerville," Vickie suggested. "It's onion ring season."

"There's an onion ring season?" I asked.

I'd never been one who ate fast food, but Vickie looked incredibly excited about it.

". Burgerville does seasonal menus, adding locally grown foods. They have these delicious Walla Walla onion rings but only in July. These are the best onion rings ever."

"Really?" I asked skeptically, unsure what could be so special about breaded onions fried in oil.

"Trust me on this. They'll change your life."

Twenty minutes later we were sitting at a picnic table in front of the burger joint eating onion rings the size of my hand. Vickie was right, these onion rings were one of the best things I'd ever eaten.

"Holy cow, these are freaking delicious," I said, grabbing another giant onion ring from the container between us. "And this burger is good too."

"Stick with me, kid, I'll show you all the finest things in life," she teased.

Suddenly I wondered, what if I had stuck with her? With the hindsight of being older and away from the relationship for a while, I couldn't help but wonder if I should have done more to try to work things out with Vickie.

I'd loved her, but she'd been pretty immature back then. My wife had been firmly anti-establishment, attending protests every weekend, getting into arguments with my friends, and sometimes doing things that were deliberately provocative. She wasted money on ridiculous things like psychics and crystals instead of saving money for retirement like I'd had drilled into my head from an early age.

But now Vickie had a nice car, a nice house, and an advanced degree that helped her move into a career that was not only satisfying, but also paid well. Somehow, I didn't think she was the same woman who flashed her boobs at cops or smoked pot while leading drum circles in her living room until two in the morning.

She'd grown up, that's for sure.

Although ten years was a long time, and I'd grown up a lot too. I'd learned to communicate instead of bottling up my feelings. I was more confident about my career and my place in the company. I was more practical about things like love and relationships.

But now, seeing the...realness of Vickie, for lack of a better term...I found myself looking at my relationship with Susannah a little differently. I'd never once considered that it had been a mistake to divorce Vickie, but I'd been pondering that exact question repeatedly since the day I went to her house to talk about the divorce. And those thoughts scared the crap out of me.

Vickie

"Are you nervous?"

I exhaled sharply. "Yeah. The last time I saw any of my family they were shouting at me about how I was going to go to hell."

I had talked to a lot of people about their coming out stories over the years; it was a common topic of conversation when people realized you were gay. For some people, their family embraced them with open arms, but too many of us were shunned, insulted, not accepted as we really were.

One of my colleagues was a youth therapist and she told me recently that while being LGBTQ was much more accepted than it was twenty years ago, there were still a lot of kids who ended up homeless because their families couldn't accept them. Like I had.

I'd been lucky to get into a program at the youth shelter in Seattle, where they gave me a safe place to stay, food to eat, and encouraged me to attend school. Too many queer youth ended up on the streets, becoming addicted to drugs or stealing to survive, some even selling their bodies.

I wasn't even sure how I'd known about the program in Seattle, but I was eternally grateful that I'd made my way up there after I left home. I was well aware that things could have turned out much worse for me than they had. It's why I made it a priority to support the homeless youth organizations in the Seattle area. I knew firsthand that the work they did was life changing.

"It sounds like your grandmother has had a pretty big change of heart since then," Claire reminded me. "I can't believe it took her five years to find you though."

"Apparently, she and the private investigator assumed I would go to Portland since it was so much closer. She told me that they were looking for me there. For some reason, it never occurred to them that I would head up north to Seattle."

"Seems like something you could clear up with a simple internet search," she sniffed. "There must be a picture of you at a party somewhere, or an Instagram post of your dinner, I mean, we all have something online anyone with an internet connection could dig up."

"I'm extremely careful about my internet presence," I explained. "I don't have any social media, and I have google alerts set up so I can clear my information from the internet when it pops up on random sites. I even bought my house through my counseling company's name."

"Why?"

I sighed deeply. "It's kind of embarrassing."

She turned in the passenger seat to face me. "Tell me. I won't judge you, I promise."

I shot her a quick look before returning my gaze to the road.

"When I was in graduate school doing my therapy practicum, I had a client get obsessed with me. I thought it was flattering, like I was really connecting with him or something, but then he started getting weird. Showing up at my job, sending me love notes, talking about us running away together, stuff like that."

"Wow."

"Yeah. I finally got freaked out enough that I went to my practicum advisor who was understandably pissed that I'd let it go on that long. I got a restraining order, and changed to a different assignment, and not that long after that he was placed in in-patient care after he had a psychotic episode and attacked someone."

"Holy shit. That could have been you."

Claire sounded concerned for me, and it made me feel a rush of warmth.

"It taught me an important lesson about privacy and professional boundaries and recognizing transference in my patients," I explained. "I've been super careful ever since. Most people have no idea how much of their private information is out there on the internet."

"Well, no Facebook post is worth getting killed over."

"Exactly."

We pulled up in front of my grandmother's house a little after two thirty. It mostly looked the same as it had when I was younger, but the yard had been neglected and the porch could use a coat of paint. Maybe I could take care of that while we were here.

Claire and I walked to the front door, and to my surprise, Claire grabbed my hand, threading her fingers through mine and giving me a squeeze. I appreciated her show of support.

An older lady answered the door with a happy smile. She looked vaguely familiar.

"Oh my god, Victoria!" The woman pulled me into a hug, practically smothering me against her bosom. "It's so good to see you again after all these years."

She released me and I gave Claire an SOS look that she clearly remembered, because she stuck out her hand and gave the woman a polite smile.

"Hi, I'm Claire, Vickie's wife."

I really loved hearing her say that.

"It's nice to meet you Claire, I'm Amy, I was Victoria's mother's best friend."

The pieces clicked. Amy had grown up next door to this house, and my mother had told me that she spent more time at Nana's house than her own, since her parents weren't around a lot.

"Do you still live next door, Amy?" I asked curiously.

The woman nodded. "Yes, I live there with my husband Earl. We try to stop by every day and make sure your Nana is doing alright. She's always been like a second mother to me."

"Well, I appreciate that Amy, thank you so much." I gave her a smile. "Where is Nana?'

"She's in the living room waiting to see you. Since you girls are here now, I'm going to head back to my place and do some laundry. But give me a holler if you need anything. Elizabeth has my number, or you can just come knock on my door."

"We will, thank you."

I walked down the hallway towards the living room, holding Claire's hand so tightly I wouldn't be surprised if I left bruises on her pale skin.

My grandmother was sitting in a recliner, a blanket around her lower body despite the fact that it was stiflingly hot in the room. Her silver and black hair was all white now, her face wrinkled, and her body was small and almost shrunken into itself.

She looked so different, yet I would have known her anywhere. When she gave me a tremulous smile and held out her arms, I dropped Claire's hand and raced across the room, dropping to my knees beside her and pulling her into a tight hug.

"Nana!"

Claire

I wasn't one who was prone to big emotions, but as I watched Vickie reunite with her grandmother, tears filled my eyes. There was so much poignancy in the moment.

I'd been fortunate when I came out to my parents that they'd taken it completely in stride. I'd worried that they'd be concerned about their social status at the country club, but fortunately two of their friends had openly gay sons, so having the first lesbian in their social group turned out to be okay in their minds.

Poor Vickie had a different experience. She'd shared the story early on in our relationship when inviting me to attend a fundraising dinner for the homeless youth shelter where she'd stayed for several years.

I knew that her Nana's rejection had impacted Vickie the most, and I was glad that the old woman was trying to make things right before she died. I just hoped she was serious about it because looking at her now, I didn't think that day was too far away.

"Hello dear, don't just stand there in the doorway."

I moved closer, walking to Vickie's grandmother's other side and offering my hand.

"Hello ma'am, my name is Claire. It's nice to meet you."

Vickie's grandmother squeezed my hand with surprising strength. "Please, call me Nana. After all, you're family."

"Thank you, Nana, and thank you for inviting us."

We spent the next hour and a half talking to Nana before she told us that she needed to go lay down for a while. Vickie and I helped her to her bedroom, tucking her into bed with the promise that we'd order pizza for dinner.

"These people around here never let me have pizza," she groused. "I'm ninety years old, I should be able to have cheesy carbs if I want, damn it."

Vickie laughed. "I'm going to order you the biggest cheesiest pizza I can find, Nana."

"Good. Now you girls make yourself at home. Amy made up the master bedroom for you, so you can put your stuff there."

"Thanks."

We grabbed our bags out of the car and took them upstairs. Nana had already mentioned that she couldn't go upstairs anymore, so I figured I could set myself up in one of the other bedrooms. It soon became apparent that my plan wasn't going to work out. In addition to the master bedroom, there were two other small bedrooms and a bathroom. One bedroom was filled almost to the ceiling with neatly stacked boxes, and the other one was completely empty, without even a stick of furniture in the room.

Vickie and I stared at the empty room for a full minute before she shrugged.

"I guess we'll have to share a bed."

For some reason she didn't look too upset about it.

"What? No. We can't do that," I protested, following her into the master bedroom.

A queen bed was set up against the wall, pillows piled up against the brass headboard. I immediately had a vision of Vickie laid out naked on the bed, her hands tied to the brass bars while I ate her out until she begged me to stop.

Damn it. This trip was bringing up too many memories. I needed to stop living in the past.

"I'm an engaged woman," I reminded both of us.

Of course, my fiancée never wanted to do anything fun like tie each other up. She was extremely vanilla. I mean sure, our sex life was nothing to write home about, but we loved each other. Or at least I thought we did. For some reason, after only six hours with Vickie, I was already questioning that belief.

"We're grown woman, I'm pretty sure we can share a bed without groping each other," Vickie said. "Quit being weird. Besides, I have a girlfriend."

I stopped dead as a wave of what I could only describe as intense jealousy roiled through me.

"What do you mean you have a girlfriend?" I asked before I could think better of it.

Vickie cocked her head, studying me. "What do you care if I have a girlfriend? We haven't seen each other in ten years."

Unable to answer that, I opened the closet and slid my bag inside, desperate for something to do beside look at Vickie standing next to a bed. I took several deep breaths before I turned to face my soon-to-be ex-wife again.

"What do you want to do while we wait for Nana to wake up?"

"I know just the thing."

An hour later I was kneeling in dirt, sweat pouring from every pore in my body while we pulled weeds in Nana's yard. I'd never seen so many weeds in my life, but Vickie was determined to clean them all out.

"It's freaking hot out here," I complained.

"It's good for you to have your hands in the soil and break a sweat," Vickie teased. "You need to get dirty every now and again."

I couldn't say what possessed me, but I picked up a handful of dirt and tossed it at her. Vickie shrieked and returned fire. The next thing I knew, we were having a dirt fight, laughing as we whipped fistfuls of dirt in each other's directions. Thanks to how sweaty we were, the dirt stuck onto our skin, turning us into muddy messes.

It was the most fun I'd had in ages.

Vickie got up and dumped two handfuls of dirt right over my head, sending a trickle of dirt right down my shirt.

I grabbed her knees, pulling her to the ground, then rolled on top of her, holding her hands on the ground by her head.

"Enough!" I laughed. "We'll never get all this dirt off us."

I looked down at Vickie's smiling face and suddenly realized that I was laying on top of her, my weight pressing her into the ground, her hands restrained. I went from zero to aroused in about a second. My nipples tightened inside my bra and the air between us became charged as we stared into each other's eyes. I had the strongest urge to kiss her.

Vickie snapped out of it first. She braced her feet on the ground and rolled until I fell off her, then jumped to her feet, reaching out a hand to help me up.

"We'd better get the garden hose," she said quietly. "Nana will kill us if we track all this dirt into the house."

Vickie

Being here with Claire and pretending to still be in a relationship was incredibly confusing. When she'd tackled me in the dirt earlier, I could have sworn she was going to kiss me. And as much as I wanted that, it would have just made this entire situation more complicated.

After we cleaned up, we ordered an obscenely large pizza and an order of hot wings – another request from Nana – and watched old movies while we ate. Nana was exactly how I remembered her from before we'd been estranged – warm and funny and a little bit wacky. I was glad to see my favorite parts of her hadn't dimmed with age.

Before we went to bed, Nana insisted that we all have a glass of raspberry brandy in the living room. We drank and reminisced about things that had happened when I was younger, a nice end to a nice day. Then Claire and I helped her get settled into her room and headed upstairs.

I whipped off my shirt, intending to change into my pajamas, and Claire gasped loudly from behind me.

"What are you doing?"

I frowned at her over my shoulder. "Getting undressed."

"I'm right here!"

"You've seen me naked a million times," I reminded her.

I'd never been particularly modest so the truth was, I wouldn't have thought twice about undressing in front of her even if we hadn't been intimate. Besides, I wasn't even facing her, the only thing she could see was my naked back and the color of my panties.

"If you're uncomfortable, I can go into the bathroom," I conceded.

"No, it's fine, I'll go," she said, walking past me towards the hallway, her own clothes in hand.

When she returned a few minutes later I was propped up against the pillows, reading a book on my iPad. Claire was wearing a tiny sleeveless nightgown that fell only a few inches down her thighs. It was white and virginal looking, with a little bow right between her breasts.

At my raised eyebrow she said, "I thought I was going to be sleeping alone."

I rolled my lips in to keep from laughing and returned to my book, although I wasn't really reading. I couldn't stop thinking about that scene in the garden earlier today, and I knew having Claire sleep next to me in her little nightgown wasn't going to help anything.

After a few minutes I gave up and went to the bathroom to get ready for bed. Turning off the light, I slipped under the sheet next to Claire. She was laying on her back, her posture stiff as she stared at the ceiling.

"Who's this woman you're dating?" she asked abruptly.

I wondered why she seemed so interested.

"Her name is Myra," I said. "She's a landscaper."

She made a grumbling noise I couldn't interpret. "How did you meet her?"

"We were both at the gardening store one day and we started talking," I said. "She asked me out to coffee afterward."

"Is it serious?"

I paused. Myra was more than a casual hook-up, but we weren't at the 'happily ever after' stage either. I couldn't imagine a long-term relationship with anyone besides Claire anyway. Really, we were more like friends with benefits, I decided.

"We haven't talked about it," I said. "We're just seeing how it goes."

When we woke up the next morning, I half expected we'd be cuddled together like always happened in the romcoms, but instead we were both hugging our respective sides of the bed, several inches of mattress between us. Bummer.

My grandmother woke up feeling particularly perky and asked if we could go for a drive.

"I want to see Mt. Hood up close again before I die," she told us, so we loaded her up in the car, crossed the river into Oregon, and drove along the Columbia Gorge Scenic Highway, which gave her a great view of both the mountain and the Gorge.

We stopped in the town of Hood River for lunch, sitting on a shaded patio facing the Columbia River where windsurfers and jet skiers were making their way across the water.

Nana seemed to be having the time of her life, talking and laughing and telling us stories from when she was young.

"I've been meaning to ask, how did you two meet?" Nana asked as we ate salmon and watched the activity on the river.

"I first saw her at a music festival on Whidbey Island," I explained. "Claire looked, well, totally out of place, but I was captivated by her beauty, so I decided to ask her to dance to see if I could loosen her up a bit. And I did."

Claire and I shared a smile.

"Vickie was this force of nature," she said softly. "So vibrant, dancing like she didn't care who was watching, living life to the fullest no matter what anyone thought. I fell in love with her the minute I set eyes on her."

We stared at each other for a long moment before turning our attention back to my grandmother.

"And you've been together ever since? That's so lovely."

"Yeah," I lied, taking a drink of my Coke to avoid looking at her. "We've had our ups and downs of course."

"That's how it is," Nana said. "I was with your grandfather for almost forty years, and I almost divorced him a dozen times. But each time we talked and worked things out and, in the end, we had a very happy life together. Communication is the key to a successful relationship, although I guess you've figured that out by now."

My eyes returned to Claire. She was looking at me with an expression I could only describe as sad. I was dying to know what she was thinking. If she regretted throwing away our relationship without trying to work things out. If she'd thought of me at all over the past ten years.

"I'm starting to get tired," Nana said, breaking my reverie. "I think it's time for you girls to take me home before I fall asleep in my chair."

Claire

"How's it going there?" Susannah asked. "Do they even have any decent restaurants in Vancouver?"

I paced on the front porch, noticing for the first time how my fiancée's voice was grating. She was acting like we were in some third world country instead of the small city that was essentially a suburb of Portland, as much as Vancouverites hated that description.

"It's going fine," I said calmly.

Susannah launched into a long description of her activities for the last two days, including such fascinating things as getting a manicure, having lunch with the wife of a tech millionaire, and testing out wedding cakes at a bakery so exclusive you had to make an appointment to get in. Why hadn't I noticed how vapid my fiancée was before? She literally said nothing interesting.

I felt a pang of shame at the thought. I mean, I had accepted Susannah's marriage proposal and committed to making a life with her. Although she'd given me a big public proposal at her family's New Year's Eve party, which had made it a little difficult to say no. Not that I wanted to say no, I reminded myself half-heartedly.

Hanging out with Vickie and eating pizza and taking drives and playing in the garden was making it painfully obvious that when I wasn't paying attention, my entire life had narrowed down to two things: work and being Susannah's arm candy.

During our time dating I'd abandoned many of my friends, primarily because Susannah didn't like them. She didn't like anyone who wasn't wealthy or well-connected. I'd also let many of my hobbies lapse. Other than working out and reading, I didn't do any of the fun activities I used to do. I couldn't remember the last time I'd gone to a movie or picked up my guitar. Instead, whenever I wasn't at work, I was basically at Susannah's beck and call.

Being with Vickie was making me question everything, including our break-up all those years ago. We'd had problems, there was no doubt about that, but Vickie had always accepted me just the way I was, and even though I hadn't done the same for her, she somehow managed to stay true to herself in the relationship.

"I still can't believe she's holding the divorce over your head to get you to do this," Susannah ranted. "She's probably still in love with you, you know. You should watch her at all times, who knows what she might do to you."

"She's my ex, Susannah, not some weird sexual predator who's going to tie me to the bed and cut off my feet so I can't escape."

"What? Why would you say something so weird?"

I repressed a sigh. Susannah got zero cultural references. Movies were too low class for her unless they were shown at the Cannes Film Festival or some similar celebrity event.

"I need to go, babe. We're helping Vickie's Nana rearrange the furniture."

"Doesn't she have people for that?" my fiancée asked.

"Yeah, us. We're the people. I'll text you later. Bye."

As the weekend progressed, I became increasingly obsessed with my soon-to-be ex-wife. It felt like everything she did was alluring. The way she ate, the way she made mumbling noises in her sleep, the skimpy clothing she wore to fight the heat, even the way she bit her lower lip when she was thinking – it was all was turning me on. I was walking around in a constant state of horniness.

My body wanted her even while my mind reminded me that I was committed to another.

While Nana napped on Sunday afternoon Vickie and I were cooking up a bunch of food to freeze for her. We figured if we stocked the freezer, when Nana wasn't feeling good, she could easily throw something in the microwave and have a nutritious meal.

We had rice going in the rice cooker, one crockpot cooking a roast while another simmered chili, and Vickie was cutting up vegetables to roast while I prepared chicken breasts to bake. It was homey and domestic, the two of us moving around the kitchen like this. We hadn't done this nearly enough when we were younger. Back then we preferred to eat out more.

"Maybe after this you can come to my house and help me stock up on prepared meals," Vickie joked. "Cooking for one isn't as much fun and I have takeout or cereal for dinner more than I'd like to admit."

"Yeah, Susannah and I eat out way too much too."

She was sitting on the counter, her feet dangling off the floor as she took a long drink from a bottle of water. Some condensation from the bottle dripped down on her chest and my eyes followed the movement of a drop of water as it slid between her breasts. She wasn't wearing a bra.

The air around us seemed to change, and I took four steps to close the distance between us. She widened her knees in an unspoken invitation, and I stepped between them, placing my hands on her naked thighs. Despite the intense heat in the kitchen, she shivered.

Vickie set the water bottle on the counter and lifted her hands to rest on my shoulders. My skin buzzed from every connection point between us. When I glanced down, Vickie's nipples were hard points against her thin tank top, and I knew mine were the same.

I shifted closer and Vickie lifted her legs, wrapping them around my hips. For a long, pregnant moment we stared into each other's eyes. She licked her lips, and my gaze fixed in that spot. I swayed closer, stopping with my lips an inch or two away from hers. Out of the corner of my eye I could see her pulse pounding in her neck.

"Vickie," I whispered, tilting my head and leaning forward to close the distance between us.

Suddenly her hand shot up, her palm covering my face as she gave me a little push backwards.

"Stop!"

Vickie

As much as it killed me to push Claire away, I knew it was the right decision.

She was engaged. I wasn't that person, and neither was she. The sexual tension had been building between us all weekend. While pretending to still be together, it made it feel like we actually were together.

I knew two things. First, I was still hopelessly in love with my wife. And second, if she betrayed her fiancée, she would never forgive herself. Or me. If we were going to explore whatever this was that was happening between us, we needed to come into it free and clear.

You have a girlfriend too, the voice in my head reminded me.

I'd nearly forgotten about Myra. We weren't super serious, but we also weren't dating other people. At least not that we'd talked about. I needed to break it off with her just in case she was more invested in our relationship than I was.

Claire stepped back, a flood of emotions passing across her face. Confusion was followed by irritation, then disappointment, and eventually relief.

"You're engaged to another woman," I reminded her. "You shouldn't be kissing me, even if we are still technically married."

"Oh God, I'm so confused," she moaned, dropping into a chair. "Being here with you is making me question everything in my life."

It was one of the most honest things she'd ever said.

I slid off the counter and stepped around her.

"Look, we're falling back into our old roles, but a lot of time has passed, and we are not the same people we were back when we were a couple. We're just...comfortable together. That's all this is."

I was lying and she knew it. It was way more than comfort or nostalgia.

"It feels like more than that," she said stubbornly. "I'm having...emotions."

Poor Claire, she'd always hated to be deep in her feelings, where as a therapist, I spent all my time analyzing my own feelings as well as the feelings of others. I couldn't help but slip into that role now.

"Tell me why you got engaged to Susannah," I said, bringing my cutting board and vegetables to the table so I could continue working while we talked.

Working with kids, I'd learned how distraction sometimes helped people open up more. Looking like you weren't listening as closely made some people feel more comfortable talking about hard things.

"Because she asked."

Claire winced as she realized how bad that sounded.

"I mean, we're mostly compatible, we get along well, and we like a lot of the same things. I don't know that I was there yet, but when she proposed at her family New Year's Eve party I kind of got caught up in the moment."

"She did a public proposal?" I asked. "You must have hated that. You don't like being the center of attention or being put on the spot to make important decisions."

Claire looked up in surprise. "Yes. See? How is it that you know that, and she doesn't?"

I shrugged, keeping my face neutral and letting her draw her own conclusions.

"What do you two do for fun?" I asked. "What are the shared activities that you both like?"

"We go to the opera, have dinner at her country club, or go shopping at boutiques," she ticked off on her fingers. "Sometimes we ride horses at her parents' country home or go skiing up on the mountain."

I dropped my knife to stare at her. There was not one thing on that list that I would have expected Claire to be interested in.

"You *enjoy* those things? Really?"

She shrugged. "Well, Susannah does, and I like to make her happy, so..."

Wow, this Susannah woman was really doing a number on her. I hated people who were controlling in relationships, it was always a red flag.

"What does she do that's just for you?" I asked, purposely keeping my tone mild.

A long silence followed. That was telling on its own, but I decided to try another direction.

"What about compatibility? Do you fight over who does the dishes or whether to put the cap on the toothpaste? Do you have similar sleep schedules? How do you divide up the chores?"

"We don't live together yet," she clarified, "so I can't really answer that. But she has a housekeeper who comes in on weekdays so things like the dishes aren't an issue."

I nodded my head. "Ah."

"Ah?" she asked. "What does that mean?"

"Nothing. It's just...I see you marrying someone who you don't really know."

She rolled her eyes. "I guess I have a habit of doing that. But I've been dating her for a year and a half, so I know her better than my last wife."

"Do you?" I asked, giving her my best therapist look.

She slumped down in her chair with a sigh but didn't answer.

"Look Claire, I'm in no position to give you advice, particularly since I'm not exactly a neutral party here, but as an old friend, I have to say, I'm concerned. Everything you've mentioned is about Susannah and what she wants, but where are you in the relationship? What do you want? You've never even said you love her."

"I love her," she said, but she sounded unconvinced. She couldn't even meet my eye when she said it.

"And does she love you?"

"I guess?" Her response came out like a question.

"You don't know?"

"Well, we don't talk about things like that," she said. "Neither of us is particularly emotional. Susannah thinks we are good partners and I...uh, I agree."

I seized on the slight hesitation. "Do you?"

"Sure."

I shook my head and went back to slicing vegetables.

"It makes me sad, Claire. You deserve real love. Big love. The kind that breaks you apart and makes you into something new and better and does the same thing for the other person. You deserve to be enjoyed and cherished. Marriage should be about love and passion and companionship, not a business merger."

Claire

Vickie's words stuck with me for the rest of the day. I was starting to realize that not only had I lost myself in my relationship with Susannah, but I'd also let her steamroll me into an engagement I wasn't sure that I wanted. God, I was so weak.

I couldn't sleep to save my life Sunday night. I kept shifting, my mind racing as I mulled over everything that had happened this weekend. My conversation with Vickie was making me see my entire relationship in a new light, and it wasn't a positive view.

After I rolled over for about the hundredth time, Vickie rolled onto her back and opened her arms.

"Come here, Claire," she said softly. "Let me help you sleep."

It wasn't sexual. I'd always had a hard time sleeping. I was a worrier and a perfectionist, and my mind was racing pretty much all the time. Early on in our relationship, I'd made the startling discovery that being cuddled by Vickie helped with my insomnia. Somehow, it quieted my mind enough to fall asleep.

I realized with a start that no one else I'd ever been with had the same effect on me, even Susannah. I scooted closer until I could rest my head on her chest, my ear right over her heart. I could hear the soft thudding through her chest. She wrapped her arms around me, and I flung one of my arms over her abdomen and tangled my legs with hers.

Immediately I felt better.

"Wow, this still works."

She lowered her head and pressed a soft kiss on the top of my hair. "Go to sleep, Claire. You don't have to figure everything out tonight."

When I woke up the next morning, I was alone in the bed. Heading downstairs, I found Vickie having coffee in the kitchen with her grandmother, the two of them talking earnestly.

"I know you like your independence, Nana, but at the point you feel like you need more help than you have now, there's an open invitation for you to come stay at my house. I have a nice sized bedroom on the first floor, right next to the bathroom."

Nana reached across the table and squeezed her hand.

"I don't deserve your kindness, Victoria, but I do appreciate it. More than you can possibly know," the older woman said. "I'm so happy that you agreed to visit me, and just thrilled that you've found the perfect woman to spend your life with. It makes me so happy seeing you two so much in love."

I cleared my throat to alert them to my presence before heading to the counter to pour myself a cup of coffee.

"How did you sleep?" Nana asked me.

My eyes flew to Vickie, and I felt a blush rising up my face. "Good, thank you."

"We're going to head out in about an hour, Nana," Vickie told her. "Is there anything else you need before we go?"

Nana shook her head. "You've given me everything I've wanted, dear, including a nicely tended garden."

After a protracted and tearful goodbye, Vickie and I got in the car and headed to the freeway to drive back up to Seattle. She was unusually quiet, with a pensive look on her face.

"How do you feel?" I finally asked after thirty minutes in the car. "Are you glad you accepted her invitation?"

She nodded. "I'm trying to decide if I should have reached out earlier."

"After the way she and your parents acted when you left, you had no way to know she'd have a change of heart. It sounds like they never did."

Death was too good for them after the way they'd treated their daughter, but I resisted mentioning that. Everything that happened led Vickie to me, and I couldn't help but be grateful for that, even though we'd split up.

"Yeah, and it sounds like for Nana it was a gradual understanding that people have different sexualities, rather than a big revelation." She glanced over at me. "The more people she knew with queers in their family, the more she realized that they were still decent people. What about you? Have you had any big revelations this weekend?"

"I have a lot of thinking to do," I evaded. I'd had many revelations, I just wasn't sure how to articulate them yet. I needed some time to process.

"I bet you do." Vickie's face was unreadable, and I was glad when she dropped the subject.

Our trip home passed faster than I expected, neither one of us saying much. By unspoken agreement, we drove all the way through without stopping, although I could have sworn that Vickie gave the Burgerville sign a longing look as we passed by Centralia.

She pulled up in front of my building, putting the car in the park and turning to face me, her expression earnest.

"Thanks for coming with me, Claire," she said. "I appreciated the moral support and all you did to help Nana. I never would have gotten all the yardwork done alone."

"No problem," I said, feeling suddenly sad that I'd probably not be seeing Vickie again. Not if I stayed with Susannah. Was I going to stay with Susannah?

Vickie studied me for a long moment.

"We were good together, Claire. I know we were young and foolish, but our relationship was based on love and passion, not convenience and social connections. You can have more. Remember that."

When I didn't respond, her face smoothed into that neutral look that she had now, her therapist look. "I'll see you later."

I stared at the side of her face for a full thirty seconds before I got out of the car. Vickie pulled away as soon as I grabbed my bag from the trunk, leaving me standing on the curb feeling more confused than I'd been in my life.

When I got upstairs to my condo, I walked around as if seeing it for the first time.

I made good money at my job at Phoenix Software, affording me the opportunity to buy a place in a nice building not that far from the office. It had a doorman, underground parking, and twenty-four hour security, all selling points for me at the time.

But as I looked around at the boring beige furniture, thick white carpeting, and stark white walls that I'd hired a decorator to design, I couldn't help but think it seemed cold. Vickie's house was warm and colorful, just like her.

I flopped down on the uncomfortable couch, staring sightlessly at an empty wall. It was a good metaphor for my life.

My phone buzzed with a message from Susannah inviting me to go out to dinner with her. By 'inviting' I meant instructing me that I was having dinner with her. Why had I allowed her to boss me around like this?

I clicked 'ignore'. I needed more time before I saw her, more time to figure out how I was feeling after being reunited with Vickie.

Unfortunately, Susannah wasn't one to be ignored. When I didn't answer her texts or subsequent phone call, she took it upon herself to come to my house. She had a key and was on the list with the doorman, so the only warning I had of her presence was the jingle of the key in the lock.

I was still on the couch, but now I was eating a bag of potato chips and drinking a beer I'd found in the far reaches of my refrigerator. Susannah looked at me in horror.

"What's wrong with you?" she asked, trying to grab the chips out of my hand.

I hugged them to my chest to keep her away from them.

"You never eat junk food. Did something happen?"

We'd been dating for two years, and she still didn't know that I had a secret stash of chips I ate when I had a bad day. That probably told me something about our relationship.

"Nothing happened," I said dully.

Never one to worry too much about anyone else or their problems, Susannah perched on a chair and started chattering about her weekend and all the important social activities she had gone to.

None of her activities had been as meaningful as reuniting an old woman with her estranged granddaughter or bringing her much-loved garden back to life.

"Put on some decent clothes," she said, her lip curling at the jeans and tee shirt I'd changed into when I got home. Susannah wouldn't be caught dead in a pair of jeans. "We'll go to Sante's for dinner."

"I don't want to go to dinner," I told her firmly. "I appreciate you coming over to check on me."

I paused, realizing that she hadn't come over to check on me, rather she couldn't stand the idea that I wasn't paying attention to her. Wow. Had she always been like this?

"Look Susannah, I just...I need some time alone. Can you please go? I'll call you tomorrow after work."

Her jaw dropped. I pretty much never said no to her.

"We're going to dinner," she said in the kind of voice a parent used with a particularly stubborn toddler. "Now, get dressed."

I looked at the woman I planned to marry and wondered what I even saw in her.

"No, we're not. You need to go now."

Vickie

"You're just going to let her go?" Myra asked.

Funny thing about my kind of girlfriend. When I told her I was going to break up with her because I was in love with someone else, she told me she was too. In love with someone else, that is.

Now we were sitting in a bar a few blocks from my house drowning our sorrows and sharing our stories of unrequited love. It was the most civilized break-up I'd ever had.

"She's engaged to another woman," I reminded Myra.

"But she's *married* to you. Married trumps engaged every time." She slammed her empty shot glass down on the table in emphasis.

"What am I supposed to do, kidnap her and hold her hostage until she agrees to get back together with me?"

"If you love her and you think she still loves you...?"

I nodded in agreement.

"You need to remind her of all the things she loved about you, all the great things you did together," Myra said. "She's probably sitting in her fancy condo with her fancy girlfriend trying to convince herself that what she's feeling is just some sentimentality about young love, brought on by forced proximity and a car trip. You need to make a statement. You need to declare your intentions and force her to face her feelings for you."

"Maybe you should take your own advice," I replied drily.

Much like Claire, Myra's lady love seemed to have no idea how Myra felt about her.

"Maybe I will."

I'd half hoped that Claire would call me, but when I went twenty-four hours without hearing from her, I decided that Myra was right. I needed to declare my intentions. I needed to make a statement. I needed to win my wife back.

Wednesday morning I sent a courier service to her office with an envelope. Inside I'd put the unsigned divorce papers, ripped into fourths.

I included a copy of the newspaper article about our wedding, with a sticky note that said:

"Claire—Fate and a clerical error gave us a second chance. Let's not waste it. Love, Vickie."

Then I had flowers delivered to her condo so they'd be waiting for her when she got home. It was a vase full of lilies, her favorite flower, and daisies, my favorite, interspersed together. I included a card that said:

"Claire – We might be very different, but we're still beautiful together. Love, Vickie."

I was disappointed when I didn't hear from her, but Myra convinced me to keep going until Claire told me to stop. I knew instinctively that if I tried hard enough, I was bound to get through to her. Or irritate her enough that she told me to stop. Either way, I'd know how she felt.

On Thursday I had Uber Eats deliver a sack full of Burgerville onion rings to her office at lunchtime, along with a cheeseburger and a strawberry shake.

When Claire got home from work on Thursday night, I had a box waiting for her with the doorman, this one full of her secret vices, including sour cream and onion potato chips, Twizzlers, a six pack of Heineken, and a DVD of *Love, Actually*. I put a silly card in the box that had a picture of two old ladies wearing bathing suits and drinking martinis. Inside the card I wrote:

"We're two of a kind. Love, Vickie".

I still hadn't heard from Claire, but I was certain she was getting my deliveries. Unless she was out of town or something, but that seemed doubtful. Claire had told me on the trip that one of the things she liked about her role as a manager was that she didn't have to travel to client sites anymore. She hated flying.

On Friday I sent a cactus with a bow to her office, along with a framed picture of us at our wedding and a note that said:

"Claire – We should do this again. Love Vickie".

I didn't know if I was getting through to her or not. Maybe she was just pitching everything in the trash, it was hard to tell without any communication back from her. I resisted texting or calling her, reminding myself that if she wanted to talk to me, she'd reach out. The ball was in her court.

By Friday night I was getting worried that my grand plan wasn't going to work.

"I haven't heard a thing from her, not a text, not an IM, nothing," I told Myra sadly. "Maybe I should just give up. She's clearly not interested."

"Don't give up. Give her time," Myra encouraged.

"Hold on a sec," I said as my doorbell rang. "I think I've got a package."

But when I opened the door, it wasn't the UPS guy, it was Claire. She was still dressed in her work clothes, looking every bit the executive with her conservative navy skirt, white blouse, and navy sling back shoes. She looked serious.

"I gotta go," I told Myra, my eyes fixed on Claire. I was afraid to blink in case I was imagining seeing her here.

"Is it her? Claire? Is she there?"

"Yeah," I said, my voice dazed. "She's here."

Myra made a whooping noise. "You get her, girl! When you come up for air, I want to hear everything."

I ended the call without saying goodbye and shoved my phone into the back pocket of my jeans. Claire was staring at me with a super intense expression that I'd never seen before. I wasn't totally sure if she was here to kill me or fuck me.

"Hey Claire," I said with forced casualness. "How's it going?"

She surged forward, grabbing my face between her hands and capturing my lips in a rough, claiming kiss. Claire kicked the door closed behind her, walking me backwards until my back slammed against the wall underneath the staircase. I was too stunned to do anything but go along with it.

She nipped at my lower lip, and when I gasped she shoved her tongue into my mouth, sliding against mine and exploring my mouth. My arms wrapped around her waist, pulling her closer. She ground her pelvis against mine, ramping up my arousal, and when she pulled away, I was both breathless and soaking wet.

"What about Susannah?" I panted.

"I broke up with her," Claire whispered.

That was all I needed to hear. This time I was the aggressor. I swung Claire around and pressed her against the wall, my hands going to the buttons of her conservative blouse, and when my fingers couldn't seem to work the buttons, I grabbed both sides and pulled, sending buttons flying. Claire gasped but I ignored her, dragging her blouse off her shoulders and reaching into her bra to pull out her left breast. I bent my knees and pulled it into my mouth, sucking on her nipple until she was making little whining noises.

"So, you're really single now?" I asked when I came up for air.

"No, I'm married. To you."

Claire

Vickie's expression turned absolutely feral.

"Get on your knees. Now."

I'd never heard this bossy voice of Vickie's, but I couldn't say that I minded it. I dropped to my knees as my wife unzipped her jeans, shoving them to her ankles, her panties soon following. Walking closer, she braced her hands on the wall and rolled her hips towards my head, bringing her pussy close to my face.

She didn't need to tell me what to do. I gripped her hips and licked my way up and down her slit a couple of times before sliding my tongue in between her folds. Vickie tasted delicious, exactly as I remembered, and I loved the fact that she was already soaking wet from our kisses.

Vickie ground her pussy against my face, dominating me while I eagerly reacquainted myself with her body. When I dipped my tongue inside her opening, she groaned loudly.

"Yes, Claire, like that."

She stepped forward, her legs on either side of my shoulders, my head trapped between her body and the wall as she dominated me. I spread her open wide with my fingers, fucking her eagerly with my tongue while she practically smothered me with her pussy. I loved it.

"Touch my clit," she ordered.

I obeyed immediately, circling and pressing her swollen bud with my thumb before pinching it between my fingers. The movement of her hips turned erratic, and I redoubled my efforts, desperate to get her off.

Suddenly Vickie stiffened against me, her body stilling for an instant before she began shaking almost violently. I shifted my hands to her hips, holding her close so I could continue servicing her with my tongue. I lapped up her cream as she cried out with her orgasm.

It had always been like this between me and Vickie. From the very first time we were together we were completely sexually compatible,

51

knowing just how to bring each other the maximum amount of pleasure every single time.

I shifted my head back, and when I looked up Vickie had her forehead pressed against the wall, her breath coming in rough pants, her hands fisted against the wall. She looked beautiful.

She sank to her knees in front of me, kissing me deeply. I knew she could taste herself on my tongue, and for some reason that turned me on even more.

When she pulled away, she whispered, "You're really free?"

"Free of everyone I want to be free of," I said.

"Good."

"What about your girlfriend?" I asked.

"We broke up. It turns out we're both in love with other people."

"You love me?" I clarified.

"I've always loved you," she said with a tender look. "Even when we were apart."

I leaned forward to press a quick kiss on her lips. "I love you too. Even before you sent me Twizzlers, I knew I could never love anyone else but you."

We were still kneeling on the floor of the entryway, and my skirt was hiked up high on my thighs from what we'd done so far. Vickie slipped her hand underneath, sliding up the skin of my inner thighs until she reached the damp barrier of my panties.

"Lay down," she said softly. "I want you too badly to make it all the way to a bed."

I couldn't say that I disagreed with that sentiment. I reached behind me to unzip my skirt, and when I shifted to the floor, Vickie helped me slide it off. My panties soon followed, leaving me wearing just a bra, with one breast in and one breast out of the cups.

"Christ, you're so beautiful." Vickie's voice was reverent.

She shifted to my side, freeing my other breast and leaning over to press a kiss to the nipple she revealed. Her breath tickled my skin.

"I didn't get to give this one any attention before," she whispered teasingly. "Let me make up for that."

I cried out as she bit down harder than I expected, sending a sting of pain right down my body. It eased into pleasure as Vickie began sucking on my aggrieved skin, smoothing her tongue over it even as she added more suction.

My back arched off the floor, and I realized I was already dangerously close to coming just from this.

Vickie's hand slid down my stomach to cup my mound, giving it a firm squeeze before sliding one finger into my wetness.

"Mine," she whispered.

I moaned in agreement. "Yours."

"You're dripping wet, you dirty girl," she teased right before she inserted a finger into my channel. "I ought to spank you for that."

I couldn't say that I was opposed to that. It had been a regular part of our bedroom activities back when we were together. I lifted my hips to meet her hand, silently begging for more, and Vickie added a second finger. She began thrusting in and out roughly while her mouth returned to teasing my breast.

"Oh my God, Vickie. I'm so close."

She lifted her head, her eyes dark with excitement.

"Then come for me, Claire. Come all over my fingers."

She grabbed the skin of my upper breast between her teeth, pinching and sucking on the sport to mark me while her fingers picked up speed deep inside my body. She found the magical spot that made pleasure crash through my body, and I shouted as I came all over her fingers just like she asked.

It was, hands down, the longest and strongest orgasm I'd had in my entire life, and even as I sagged against the floor in release, my pussy was still twinging with little electrical pulses.

"I love you," I gasped. "I love you so much, Vickie."

"I love you too," she replied. "I never stopped loving you."

Vickie rolled us both to our sides, pulling me into her arms, and we stared into each other's eyes, huge smiles on our faces.

"I hope this means that we're getting back together now," Vickie told me firmly. "You'll move in here, of course. I can't live in that cold, soulless condo of yours."

"You've never even been inside," I protested.

"I don't need to be. I just know."

She shuddered, as if she was picturing my place as some kind of house of horrors instead of a very expensive condo in an exclusive neighborhood.

"Well, fortunately for you I like your place better anyway," I responded.

We snuggled a bit longer then got up and made our way up the stairs to Vickie's bedroom where we made each other come again and again, trying to make up for ten years of lost time.

"What do you think about renewing our vows?" I asked later that night as we ate Chinese takeout naked in bed.

"You want to do that?" she asked in surprise.

"It seems like the right thing to do. Plus, it might be nice for Nana since she missed our first wedding. We could have the ceremony in Vancouver if you want."

"Let's do it. A new ceremony for our new start."

Vickie put her container of food on the table, then grabbed mine and put it there too. Pulling me into her arms, she gave me a long, hard kiss.

"I'm so glad we got our second chance, Claire."

"Me too, love. Let's make this one stick."

Epilogue – Vickie

Five months later...

"Are you sure this outfit is okay?" I asked, gesturing at the dress I was wearing for the big holiday party at Phoenix Technology.

The event was going to be held at a nice restaurant, and while I'd met several of Claire's coworkers since we'd been back together, this was going to be our first non-casual event. I kept thinking back to the last fancy affair we'd attended together, the one where I'd embarrassed Claire and convinced her that we were never going to work out together.

I remember getting into an argument about global warming with some rich old white guy who was an investor in the company. This time I planned to steer clear of any potentially controversial topics.

Then again, Claire was much more secure in her role in the company now, and less worried about what people thought. Plus, I'd learned to keep my trap shut as I got older. Not everything needed to be a battle, I knew that now.

"You look beautiful," Claire told me. "Especially with that new ring on your finger."

Claire and I had renewed our vows over Thanksgiving weekend. We'd brought Nana up to stay with us and invited her to stay until New Year's. We all knew that she didn't have much time left, and Claire and I were trying to convince her to move in with us full-time so we could spend however much time she had left together.

"I don't mind seeing that big rock on your finger either, wifey," I teased, gesturing at the diamond ring that I'd purchased for her.

We'd been living together for five months now, and I'd frankly been surprised how easy it was. Claire and I had both grown up a lot over the last decade, and while we had love on our side the first time around, now our relationship was also built on respect, maturity, and friendship.

There was no cleaning lady picking up after us like she would have had if she'd married Susannah, but Claire didn't seem to mind sharing the housekeeping and chores.

As we pulled out of the driveway to head to the Christmas party, Claire said out of the blue, "What do you think about becoming foster parents?"

I stopped the car, putting it in park, and turned to stare at her in surprise. "What?"

"Well, I was thinking it would be good to have a kid, but we're both in our mid-thirties so it might be safer to adopt. But then that made me think about all the kids in foster care. We both have good jobs so we can take care of some kids and provide them with a good life. What do you think?"

I grabbed Claire's hand and pulled it to my mouth, laying a kiss on her knuckles.

"I think we'd make great parents, no matter what option we decide, because we'd love them as much as we love each other."

"We will. We will make it our mission to show them love, no matter where they came from."

And as we opened our house to kids over the years, we did.

***

Want to read about Claire's friends and coworkers as they find love with the women they were meant to spend their lives with? Check out the rest of the "Friends to Lovers" series today.
You can find more of Reba's lesbian romances at
Books2read.com/rl/lesbianromance[1]
If you liked this book, please consider leaving a review or rating to let me know.
Be sure to join my newsletter for more great books. You'll receive a free book when you join my newsletter. Subscribers are the first to hear about

---

1. *https://books2read.com/rl/lesbianromance*

all of my new releases and sales. Visit my mailing list sign-up at bit.ly/ RebaBaleSapphic[2] to download your free book today.

Special Preview

The Divorcee's First Time
A Contemporary Lesbian Romance
By Reba Bale

"It's done," I said triumphantly. "My divorce is final."

My best friend Susan paused in the process of sliding into the restaurant booth, her sharply manicured eyebrows raising almost to her hairline. "Dickhead finally signed the papers?" she asked, her tone hopeful.

I nodded as Susan settled into the seat across from me. "The judge signed off on it today. Apparently his barely legal girlfriend is knocked up, and she wants to get a ring on her finger before the big event." I explained with a touch of irony in my voice. "The child bride finally got it done for me."

Susan smiled and nodded. "Well congratulations and good riddance. Let's order some wine."

We were most of the way through our second bottle when the conversation turned back to my ex. "I wonder if Dickhead and his Child Bride will last for the long haul," Susan mused.

I shook my head and blew a chunk of hair away from my mouth.

"I doubt it," I told her. "Someday she's gonna roll over and think, there's got to be something better out there than a self-absorbed man child who doesn't know a clitoris from a doorknob."

Susan laughed, sputtering on her wine. I eyed her across the table. Although she was ten years older than me, we had been best friends for the last five years. We worked together at the accounting firm. She had been my trainer when I first came there, fresh out of school with my degree. We bonded over work, but soon realized that we were kindred spirits.

Susan was rapidly approaching forty but could easily pass for my age. Her hair was black and shiny, hinting at her Puerto Rican heritage, with blunt bangs and blond highlights that she paid a fortune for. Her face was clear and unlined, with large brown eyes and cheek bones that could cut glass. She was an avid runner and worked hard to maintain a slim physique since the women in her family ran towards the chunkier side.

I was almost her complete opposite. Blonde curls to her straight dark hair, blue eyes instead of brown, curvy where she was lean, introverted to her extrovert.

But somehow, we clicked. We were closer than sisters. Honestly, I don't know how I would have gotten through the last year without her. She had been the first one I called when my marriage fell apart, and she had supported me throughout the whole process.

It had been a big shock when I came home early one day and found my husband getting a blow job in the middle of our living room. It had been even more shocking when I saw the fresh young face at the other end of that blow job.

"What the fuck are you doing?" I had screeched, startling them both out of their sex stupor. "You're getting blow jobs from children now?"

The girl had looked up from her knees with eyes glowing in righteous indignation. "I'm not a child, I'm nineteen," she had informed me proudly. "I'm glad you finally found out. I give him what you don't, and he loves me."

I looked into the familiar eyes of my husband and saw the panic and confusion there. I made it easy for him. "Get out," I told him firmly, my voice leaving no room for argument. "Take your teenage girlfriend and get the fuck out. We're getting a divorce. Expect to hear from my lawyer."

The condo was in my name. I had purchased it before we were married, and since I had never added his name to the deed, he had no rights to it. There was no question he would be the one leaving.

My husband just stared at me with his jaw hanging open like he couldn't believe it. "But Jennifer," he whined. "You don't understand. Let me explain."

"There's nothing to understand," I told him sadly. "This is a deal breaker for me, and you know that as well as I do. We are done."

The girl had taken his hand and smiled triumphantly. "Come on baby," she told him. "Zip up and let's get out of here. We can finally be together like we planned."

"Yeah baby," I had sneered. "I'll box up your stuff. It'll be in the hallway tomorrow. Pick it up by six o'clock or I'm trashing it all."

After they left my first call was to the locksmith, but my second call was to Susan.

That night was the last time I had seen my husband until we had met for the court-ordered pre-divorce mediation. He spent most of that session reiterating what he had told me in numerous voice mails, emails and sessions spent yelling on the other side of my front door. He loved me. He had made a terrible mistake. He wasn't going to sign the papers. We were meant to be together. Needless to say, mediation hadn't been very successful. Fortunately, I had been careful to keep our assets separate, as if I knew that someday I would be in this situation.

Through it all, Susan had been my rock. In the end I don't think I was even that sad about the divorce, I was really angrier with myself for staying in a relationship that wasn't fulfilling with a man I didn't love anymore.

"You need to get some quality sex." Susan drew my attention back to the present. "Bang him out of your system."

"I don't know," I answered slowly. "I think I need a hiatus."

"A hiatus from what?" Susan asked with a frown. "You haven't had sex in what, eighteen months?"

I nodded. "Yeah, but I just can't take a disappointing fumble right now. I would rather have nothing than another three-pump chump."

I shook my head and continued, "I'm going to stick with my battery-operated boyfriend, he never disappoints me."

Susan smiled. "That's because you know your way around your own vajayjay."

She motioned to the waiter to bring us a third bottle of wine.

"That's why I like to date women," she continued. "We already know our way around the equipment."

I nodded thoughtfully. "You make a good point."

Susan leaned forward. "We've never talked about this," she said earnestly. "Have you ever been with a woman?"

For more of the story, check out "The Divorcee's First Time" by Reba Bale, available for immediate download[1] today.

***

Want a free book? Join my newsletter and a special gift. I'll contact you a few times a month with story updates, new releases, and special sales. Visit bit.ly/RebaBaleSapphic[2] for more information.

---

1.   https://books2read.com/u/bpznKX

2. https://bit.ly/RebaBaleSapphic

Other Books by Reba Bale

Check out my other books, available on most major online retailers now. Go to my webpage[1] at bit.ly/AuthorRebaBale to learn more.

Friends to Lovers Lesbian Romance Series
    The Divorcee's First Time
    My BFF's Sister
    My Rockstar Assistant
    My College Crush
    My Fake Girlfriend
    My Secret Crush
    My Holiday Love
    My Valentine's Gift
    My Spring Fling
    My Forbidden Love
    My Office Wife
    My Second Chance
    Coming Out in Ten Dates
    Worth Waiting For

The Club Surrender Series
Jaded
Hated
Fated
Saved
Caged

The Second Chances Lesbian Romance
Last Christmas
The Summer I Fell in Love

---

1. https://books2read.com/ap/nB2qJv/Reba-Bale

Sapphic Security

Guarding the Senator's Daughter

Menage Romances

Pie Promises

Tornado Warning

Summer in Paradise

Life of the Mardi

Bases Loaded

Two For One Deal

The Unexpectedly Mine Series

Sinful Desires

Taken by Surprise

Just One Night

Forbidden Desires

Hotwife Erotic Romances

Hotwife in the Woods

Hotwife on the Beach

Hotwife Under the Tree

A Hotwife's Retreat

Hot Wife Happy Life

Want a free book? Just join my newsletter at bit.ly/RebaBaleSapphic[2]*.*
You'll be the first to hear about new releases, special sales, and free
offers.

---

2. https://bit.ly/RebaBaleSapphic

About the Author

Reba Bale writes erotic romance, lesbian romance, menage romance, & the spicy stories you want to read on a cold winter's night. When Reba is not writing she is reading the same naughty stories she likes to write.

You can also follow Reba on Medium[3] for free stories, bonus epilogues and more. You can also hear all about new releases and special sales by joining Reba's newsletter mailing list.[4]

Don't miss out!

Visit the website below and you can sign up to receive emails whenever Reba Bale publishes a new book. There's no charge and no obligation.

https://books2read.com/r/B-A-IDTM-QSOSC

BOOKS 2 READ

Connecting independent readers to independent writers.

Milton Keynes UK
Ingram Content Group UK Ltd.
UKHW010956080124
435661UK00001B/143